Enjoy !!

Pat Lopez

To all my wonderful grandchildren:
Anna, who helped create this story;
Sammi, who inspired this story;
Max and Emily, who listened many times;
And to all the girls with RETT
Syndrome who struggle every day.

Library of Congress Control Number: 2012933177

ISBN-13: 9781937406813
ISBN-10: 1937406814

www.mascotbooks.com

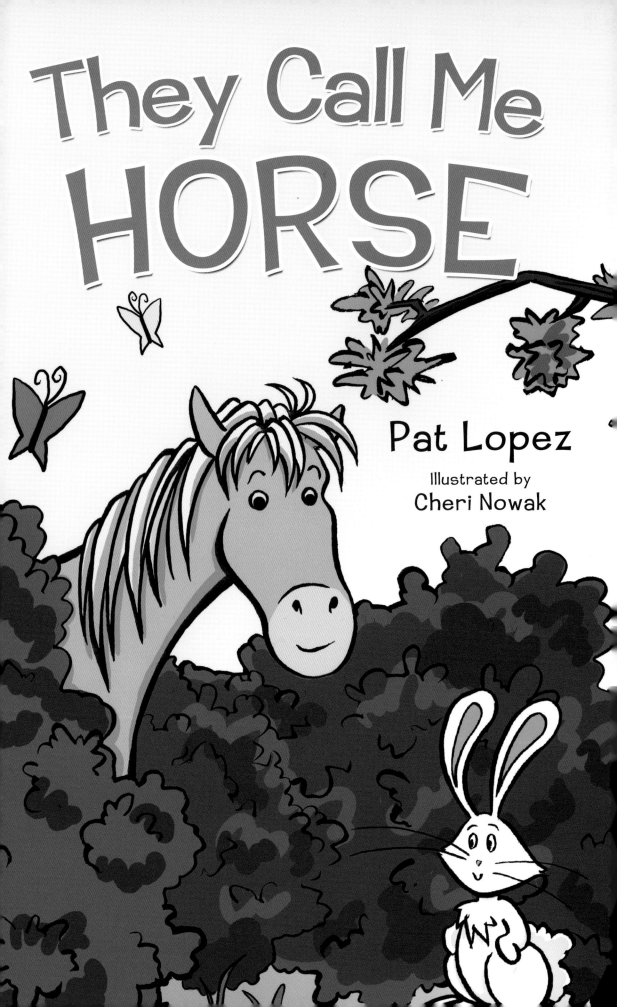

They Call Me HORSE

Pat Lopez

Illustrated by
Cheri Nowak

I am called horse. I guess because I am a horse! Most other animals have names, but I don't and that makes me sad.

One day, I decided to go for a walk in the forest to think about a name. As I walked, I saw a rabbit and she was crying.

I asked, "Why are you crying?"

She told me, "My playmates call me names." I couldn't understand why anyone would cry about being called names because I wanted one so badly.

She explained, "They are not nice names, they are 'being mean' names."

I told her, "I am sorry they did that. I would like to be your friend. I don't have a name. Can you help me find a name?"

"Yes, that would make me very happy," she said. "My name is Fluffy."

As we walked, we met a frog. He was hopping in circles. We stopped to ask why he was hopping in circles.

He said, "I am having a problem with one of my legs and I can't hop straight."

Fluffy rubbed his leg and he stopped hopping in circles. "My name is Freddy and thank you for your help," he said. We asked Freddy if he would like to come with us. He was so happy that he hopped very high.

I told Freddy, "I'm not being rude by not telling you my name, but I don't have one." He and Fluffy came up with all kinds of names: Harry, Joey, and Spice. We agreed that none of them were quite right.

We continued on our way and met a squirrel who was digging holes everywhere. He was very upset.

He said, "I can't remember where I buried my food for the winter."

I told him, "I can help by banging against the trees and knocking down nuts and berries."

He replied, "I'm Sam and I am so happy for your help." Sam buried all the nuts and berries in the holes he already dug. Sam decided to come with us and he wanted to help me find a name. He thought of Mike, Max, and Power, but they weren't right.

We were getting thirsty and found a pond.
In the pond was a strange looking bird. We
didn't know what it was.

It had gray feathers and a long neck. It swam up to us and said, "Hello, my name is Sara and I am a swan. I don't have my beautiful white feathers yet so I don't look like a swan." Sara was lonely because she was the only swan left in the pond. All the other swans had flown to the big lake and she couldn't fly yet. I asked Sara, "How long will it be before you get your grown-up feathers to fly with?" Sara told us, "Just a few weeks." We asked if she would like to come with us. Sara couldn't walk as well as everyone else. She was made to swim and fly, so she got on my back and got a ride.

We continued to walk and saw a fox chasing a little mouse.

I stood in front of the fox and said, "Leave the mouse alone!" The fox got scared because I am so big.

Sara, Sam, and Fluffy told him not to be scared because I was a friend.

The fox said, "This is only a game I play with the smaller animals."

I knew the small animals were scared, so I told him it wasn't nice. I asked him, "How would you feel if I chased you as a game?"

The fox said I was right, but there wasn't anyone else to play with. "I'm Red," he said. "Can I go with you?"

We all replied, "Sure!"

As we walked, we started to get cold. We knew it was going to be dark soon and it was too late to go home. We looked for a place to spend the night and saw a barn in the distance.

When we got to the barn there was a cow that lived there. I asked him, "Could we spend the night here?" He said, "I'm Bob and the man who owns the farm wouldn't mind at all." We told Bob about our adventure. Bob said it must have been very exciting for us. I told him, "This started out with me trying to find a name and along the way I met wonderful friends, but I still don't have a name."

Bob looked at me and started to laugh. "Why, that is the easiest thing! You are tan with brown and black patches. Patches should be your name."
I was so excited! I loved my name!
"Patches is a great name!" Everyone agreed that it was perfect. Bob, being very smart, told us that

we were more than friends. After all we shared, we were more like a family. Remember what Patches and his friends learned the next time you see someone that looks different. Even though we look different, we all have the same feelings and needs. Patches and his friends proved that.

The End

About the Author

I am the grandma to a little girl, Sammi, who has RETT Syndrome (a degenerative neurological disorder). Because of that, she can look and act different. This story was written to help others understand she has the same feelings and needs as everyone else. Our journeys in life change, just like horse and his friends.

Have a book idea?

Contact us at:

**Mascot Books
560 Herndon Parkway
Suite 120
Herndon, VA 20170**

info@mascotbooks.com | www.mascotbooks.com